Today Is Easter!

Written and illustrated by
P.K. Hallinan

FOREST HOUSE ™
School & Library Edition

*For John, David, Christine,
and Mariah Applegate*

FOREST HOUSE ™

This 1993 School and Library Edition published by FOREST HOUSE PUBLISHING COMPANY, INC.

Printed and bound in the United States of America.

Forest House Publishing Co., Inc.
P. O. Box 738
Lake Forest, IL 60045

ISBN **1-878363-94-8**

Publisher's Cataloging-in-Publication Data

Hallinan, P. K.
    Today is Easter! / Written and illustrated
by P. K. Hallinan.
                    p.   cm.
    Summary: A small child celebrates Easter
and learns that there is more to this holiday
than just candy and colored eggs.
        ISBN 1-878363-94-8
        1. Easter--Fiction 2. Stories in rhyme
I. T
PZ7.H38T62   1993   [E]   CIP

It's Easter today
and the sun's gentle light
sifts through your window
and lifts up the night.

What a glorious day!
What a beautiful dawn!
You climb out of bed
with a stretch and a yawn.

For outside your window
songbirds are singing,
and from down in the town,
you hear chapel bells ringing.

And the lilies adorn
this lavender morn.

You put on your slippers
and head down the stairs
to see what the Easter Bunny
left for you there.

And it doesn't take long
to find your surprise—
a basket of candy
bedazzles your eyes!

And oh, what a scene!
It's a jelly bean dream!

But now your excitement
soars clear out of sight,
as you search for the eggs
that you colored last night.

There's one over here!
And two over there!
And four, maybe more,
at the foot of the stairs!

So hurry—get dressed!
Wear your new Easter best.
Just zip what you have to
and button the rest!

And with time running low, you're ready to go.

The steps of the church
are alive with the sound
of nice people talking
and walking around.

And everyone smiles
and nods as they say,
"My, but it's lovely
to see you today!"

And you happily share
all the fellowship there.

There are women in sashes
and men in felt hats.
There are girls wearing curls
and chaps in cravats.

And the flowers are blooming
like never before
to add to the gladness
of this Easter decor.

The sermon is stirring and tells of the glory of Christ's Resurrection, of Easter's first story.

And everyone rises
together and sings
a thank-you to Easter
for the hope that it brings.

Then with deep, loving care,
you all join in prayer.

At midafternoon
there are games with balloons,
while nearby the band
plays grand little tunes.

At home you sit down
to a wonderful fare
of laughter and friendship
with people who care.

And hands join together
as all hearts embrace
the joy of this moment
with an Easter Day grace.

Then with blessings complete,
you're ready to eat!

Too soon the day wanes
like a ticktocking clock,
and your energy sags
like a baggy old sock.

So you hop in your jammies
and drop into bed,
as the day slowly sways
and replays in your head.

And the last thing you say
before fading away is